Tom and Pippo's Day,
Tom and Pippo and the Washing Machine,
Tom and Pippo Read a Story,
Tom and Pippo Make a Mess and
Tom and Pippo See the Moon first published 1988
Pippo Gets Lost first published 1989
by Walker Books Ltd, 87 Vauxhall Walk, London SE11 5HJ

This edition published 1995

10 9 8 7 6 5 4 3 2 1

© 1988, 1989 Helen Oxenbury

This book has been typeset in Stempel Schneidler Medium.

Printed in Hong Kong

British Library Cataloguing in Publication Data
A catalogue record for this book is
available from the British Library.

ISBN 0-7445-3776-2 (hb)
ISBN 0-7445-3721-5 (pb)

SIX TODDLER STORIES

At Home with TOM AND PIPPO

Helen Oxenbury

WALKER BOOKS
AND SUBSIDIARIES
LONDON · BOSTON · SYDNEY

Tom
and
Pippo's
Day

When I wake up
early in the morning,
first I give Pippo
a hug.

Then we go to see
if Mummy and Daddy
are awake.

Daddy has to hurry with
his breakfast. Sometimes
I give Pippo some
of mine, but he's
so clumsy and
he makes a mess.

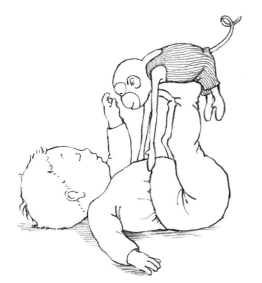

Pippo and I do things together all day, until Daddy comes home.

When it's bedtime, I sometimes don't know where Pippo is and I have to look everywhere until I find him.

9

Because when
it's time to go
to sleep, I need
to be with
Pippo.

Tom and Pippo and the Washing Machine

One day Pippo played in the mud and got really dirty. Mummy said we would have to put him in the machine with the washing.

I said goodbye to Pippo because
I thought he might never
come out of the machine.

Poor Pippo went
round and round.
I hoped he didn't feel
sick. When Pippo came
out of the machine,
he was really wet.

"Will Pippo ever get dry?"
I asked Mummy. Mummy said
he'd soon be dry if he went on
the line with the washing.

I told Pippo he'd
be dry by bedtime
if the sun came
out and the wind
kept blowing.

13

The trouble is,
I know Pippo's
going to get dirty
again. I can't stop
him playing in
muddy places.

Tom and Pippo Make a Mess

When Daddy is at home I watch the way he does things and I try to do the same.

 When Daddy writes a letter I go and get my pen and write a letter too. When Daddy shaves, I pretend I'm shaving. Pippo thinks I shouldn't waste the shaving cream.

 One day Daddy was doing some painting. While he was out of the room I did some painting to help him.

Daddy said I had made a mess and he was cross.

Anyway, it was Pippo who said we should help Daddy, and I had to be cross with him.

Daddy said
he is going to
work in the
garden tomorrow.
I hope he wants
me to help.

Pippo Gets Lost

Sometimes Pippo gets lost and I have to look for him.

I asked Mummy if she'd
seen Pippo, and she said
I should look again in
the toy-box. Pippo wasn't
there, but I found his scarf.

Daddy said, "Have you looked
under your bed?" But all I found
there was Pippo's hat. I got really
worried about Pippo and thought
I might never see him again.

Mummy said Pippo couldn't be far away and we should look in the sitting room. And that's where he'd been all the time, in the bookcase.

If Pippo is going
off on his own,
I've told him he
really should
let me know.

Tom and Pippo Read a Story

I like to look at books,
but best of all I like to
look at books with Daddy.

Daddy likes to look
at his paper, but he
doesn't mind reading
my books to me.
When Daddy's
finished reading to me,
I think Pippo would like
to hear a story. So I bring
Pippo and ask Daddy
to read to him.

When Daddy says he really
can't read any more books,
I read to Pippo.

I hope one day
Pippo can read
on his own.

Tom
and
Pippo
See the
Moon

One night when it was dark, I saw the moon shining in the sky.

I asked Daddy all about the moon.
Daddy told me a man had been on the
moon and he had to get there in a rocket.
I asked Daddy if there was anybody
on the moon now, and
Daddy said no.
I think Pippo and I
will go to the moon
one day. We will
go in a rocket.

I asked Daddy if Pippo and I could go to the moon, and Daddy said maybe, but the moon is very far away.

If Pippo and I go to the moon one day, I think Daddy should come as well.

Anyway,
tonight I think
we will just go
to sleep. Perhaps
we will go to the
moon tomorrow.

MORE WALKER PAPERBACKS
For You to Enjoy

Growing up with Helen Oxenbury

TOM AND PIPPO

There are six stories in each of these two colourful books about
toddler Tom and his special friend Pippo, a soft-toy monkey.

"Just right for small children… A most welcome addition to the nursery shelves." *Books for Keeps.*

At Home with Tom and Pippo   0-7445-3721-5
Out and About with Tom and Pippo   0-7445-3720-7
£3.99 each

THREE PICTURE STORIES

Each of the titles in this series contains three classic stories of pre-school life,
first published individually as First Picture Books.

"Everyday stories of family life, any one of these humorous depictions of
the trials of an under five will be readily identified by children and adults …
buy them all if you can." *Books For Your Children*

One Day with Mum   0-7445-3722-3
A Bit of Dancing   0-7445-3723-1
A Really Great Time   0-7445-3724-X
£3.99 each

MINI MIX AND MATCH BOOKS

Originally published as Heads, Bodies and Legs these fun-packed
little novelty books each contain 729 possible combinations!

"Good value, highly imaginative, definitely to be looked out for." *Books For Your Children*

Animal Allsorts   0-7445-3705-3
Puzzle People   0-7445-3706-1
£2.99 each